ana &
ANDREW

Dancing at Carnival

by Christine Platt
illustrated by Sharon Sordo

Calico Kid

An Imprint of Magic Wagon
abdobooks.com

For Granny Pam, Grandpa Thom, Royce and Renae. —CP

For Logan, May your life be an exciting party, full of joy and books. —SS

abdobooks.com

Published by Magic Wagon, a division of ABDO, PO Box 398166, Minneapolis, Minnesota 55439. Copyright © 2019 by Abdo Consulting Group, Inc. International copyrights reserved in all countries. No part of this book may be reproduced in any form without written permission from the publisher. Calico Kid™ is a trademark and logo of Magic Wagon.

Printed in the United States of America, North Mankato, Minnesota.
102018
012019

 THIS BOOK CONTAINS
RECYCLED MATERIALS

Written by Christine Platt
Illustrated by Sharon Sordo
Edited by Tamara L. Britton
Art Directed by Candice Keimig

Library of Congress Control Number: 2018947938

Publisher's Cataloging-in-Publication Data

Names: Platt, Christine, author. | Sordo, Sharon, illustrator.
Title: Dancing at carnival / by Christine Platt; illustrated by Sharon Sordo.
Description: Minneapolis, Minnesota : Magic Wagon, 2019. | Series: Ana & Andrew
Summary: It's Spring Break! During Carnival, Ana & Andrew travel to visit their family on the island of Trinidad. They love watching the parade and dancing to the music. This year, they learn how their ancestors helped create the holiday!
Identifiers: ISBN 9781532133510 (lib. bdg.) | ISBN 9781532134111 (ebook) | ISBN 9781532134418 (Read-to-me ebook)
Subjects: LCSH: Family vacations–Juvenile fiction. | Families–History–Juvenile fiction. | Carnival–Juvenile fiction. | African American history–Juvenile fiction.
Classification: DDC [E]–dc23

Table of Contents

Chapter #1
We've Got Mail!

Ana and Andrew checked the mailbox every day. It was one of their favorite chores. There were always envelopes for Papa and Mama. But sometimes, Ana and Andrew received mail too. They loved getting cards on their birthdays and special holidays.

And every spring, they looked forward to receiving a letter from their cousin, Michael, who lived in Trinidad.

One day, Ana and Andrew opened the mailbox and saw a letter addressed to them. It was written in Michael's handwriting. "We've got mail!" Andrew did a wiggle-dance.

Ana laughed. "Open it!"

Andrew opened the letter very carefully and read the note that was inside:

Dear Ana and Andrew,

It's time for Carnival!
This year our costumes
are very funny. I hope you
like them!

See you soon!

Your cousin,
Michael

ME ANA ANDREW

Every Carnival, Ana and Andrew visited their family on the island of Trinidad where there are lots of beaches and seashells. Carnival was a big party. Everyone dressed up in costumes they called '*mas*,' and danced with their family and friends.

Ana and Andrew looked at the letter and smiled. They couldn't wait to leave for Trinidad!

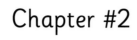

Chapter #2
Hello, Trinidad

Ana and Andrew looked out the airplane window.

"Look at all of that water," Andrew said. "It's so blue!"

"And it's so pretty." Ana smiled and held up her dolly, Sissy, so she could see too.

"Ah, it feels good to be back." Mama grew up in Trinidad. She loved showing Ana and Andrew where she went to school and played when she was a girl.

"The ocean sure is beautiful." Papa held Mama's hand.

Ana and Andrew got off the plane with their parents. Then they went to baggage claim to get their luggage. As they picked up their suitcases, Ana and Andrew heard a familiar laugh. They turned around excitedly.

"Cousins!" Michael laughed. "What a go on?"

Ana and Andrew loved Michael's accent. People in Trinidad spoke differently than people in Washington, DC. Everyone in Trinidad talked like Mama—every word sounded like a song.

"It's great to see you." Mama hugged Michael. "You've gotten so tall."

Michael stood proudly. "Thank you, Tanty." That was what people in Trinidad called their aunts.

"Now where is that brother of mine?" Mama looked around the airport.

Suddenly, two strong arms picked up Ana and Andrew. "Uncle Errol!" they squealed.

Everyone hugged each other. It always felt good to be with family.

Chapter #3
Family Fun

Ana and Andrew enjoyed playing with Michael and his friends that evening. And the adults enjoyed spending time with Michael's new baby sister, Amada.

The next morning, everyone went to the beach. After swimming in the ocean, Ana and Andrew ate one of their favorite island snacks called the doubles.

They loved the taste of curried beans wrapped in a sweet dough. After swimming a bit more, everyone went home for dinner.

"I am so excited about Carnival," Ana said. "I cannot wait for Sissy to see the parade and dance to the music."

"Yes, it's always a grand celebration," Papa said. "And so colorful. I think Sissy is going to love it."

"I definitely love it!" Andrew did a wiggle-dance and everyone laughed. "Who started this Carnival party?" Andrew wanted to know.

"That's a very good question," Uncle Errol said. "Let me tell you how it all began."

Ana and Andrew moved closer to Uncle Errol and listened.

"Many years ago, there were slaves on the island of Trinidad, just like there were in America. These slaves were our ancestors.

"Slave owners used to have grand parties called masquerades, where they dressed up in costumes. But our ancestors were not allowed to attend the slave owners' parties," Uncle Errol explained.

"Maybe the slaves didn't want to go to those parties." Ana thought about what she learned about slavery in school. She couldn't imagine slaves and slave owners at a party together.

"That is possible," Uncle Errol said. "And perhaps that is why our ancestors created their own masquerade party. Carnival!"

"I get it!" Andrew shouted. "*Mas* is short for masquerade. That's why everyone wears costumes!"

"That's right!" Uncle Errol smiled.

"Speaking of costumes . . ." Aunt Renee walked into the living room carrying a big box. Ana and Andrew ran to see what was inside.

"Oh my!" Ana laughed as she pulled out a large green wig. Andrew pulled out a red rubber nose and put it on.

"That's right," Michael said. "We're going to be clowns!" There was a small costume for his baby sister, Amada. And an even smaller costume for Sissy.

"Now off to bed," Papa said.

"Tomorrow's the big day!"

Ana and Andrew could hardly sleep
because they were so excited.

Chapter #4
Party Time!

The next morning everyone ate breakfast. Then it was time to get dressed.

First, they put on their baggy pants, shirts, and bow ties. Next, they put on their colorful wigs. Ana couldn't stop laughing at Andrew's purple wig. Then, everyone put on a pair of big, floppy shoes.

"We look just like clowns," Andrew said.

"We *are* clowns!" Michael put red noses on Ana and Andrew. The three cousins looked in the mirror and danced around like clowns. Then they went outside with their parents to join the parade.

There were so many different costumes. Some people were dressed as bats and dragons.

Others were dressed up as baby dolls. And some men were dressed up as warriors.

Many of the women wore headpieces made with colorful features that matched their costumes.

Children played steel drums and everyone danced to the music.

"Hey, I almost forgot something!"
Michael ran up to Andrew and put a
crown on his head.

"What's this?" Andrew asked.

"Why, you're the King Clown,
course." Michael bowed to Andrew.
"You're the leader of our band. And
now, it's party time!"

"Aye!" Andrew did a wiggle-dance and everyone laughed. Then they followed Andrew down the street as they danced and prepared to have fun dancing at Carnival.